Sweety

Andrea Zuill

schwartz & wade books · new york

Sweety was awkward.
Even for a naked mole rat.*

(*Please note that naked mole rats are born without fur but not without the love of clothes.
The illustrator is grateful for this since she didn't have to draw a bunch of highly embarrassing pictures.)

Her own grandmother called her a little square peg.
Sweety didn't exactly know what that meant.

But she did know that she didn't always fit in.

Sweety could be intense.

And people found her
hobbies a bit bizarre.

Occasionally Sweety did things that others had a hard time comprehending. Like the day she gave her book report through interpretive dance.

There were times when Sweety wondered what it would be like to be someone else. Someone like Deb. Deb always said the right thing and had stylish friends. Best of all, she had beautiful hair. Sweety wanted hair like Deb's.

Deb's hair

Deb

She thought maybe she should try a wig.

Then there were times when Sweety just felt like being Sweety.

The best days were when Aunt Ruth visited.
Aunt Ruth understood Sweety perfectly.

She didn't think Sweety's hobbies were weird.

Really, not a single one.

Ann and Ruth, 2 sassy cowgir

Sweety and her aunt loved going through
old family photo albums. Sweety especially
liked the pictures of her mom and her aunt
when they were her age.

On her most recent visit, Aunt Ruth talked about
how she was called a square peg when she was young.
Sweety was starting to understand what that meant.

Aunt Ruth said that being different was one of the best things about her life, and that if you stayed true to yourself, you'd find your people.

That made Sweety think.

Were there really people out there for her?
How would they recognize her? How would she
recognize them? Was there a secret handshake
she'd have to learn?

She really hoped there was a secret handshake.

Sweety wondered how many times she'd been
close to one of her people and not known it.

What if she stepped it up a notch? Would her people be able to spot her more easily?

My name is Sweety. I like dancing, mushrooms, and rainy days. You too? Need to find your people? Maybe we're a match! Flyers are available.

Or would she just seem desperate?

For now, she'd trust Aunt Ruth, continue to do her favorite things, and be herself.

And maybe she'd try
a couple of new hobbies
just for fun.

After all, being Sweety wasn't so bad.

In fact, it could be pretty awesome.

And who knew when someone else pretty awesome might come along?

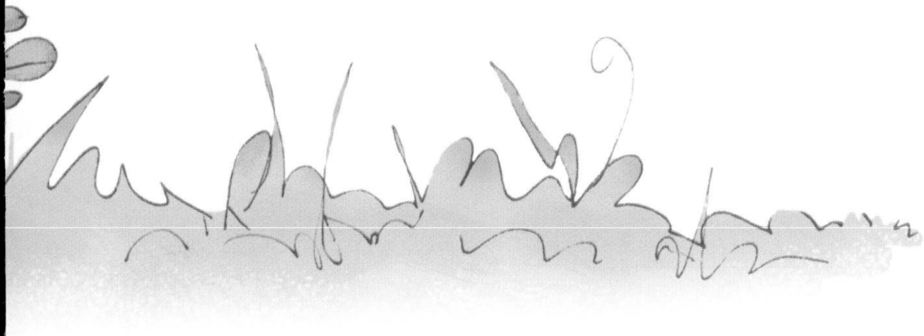

For all those who have accepted their inner oddball

All rights reserved. Published in the United States by Schwartz & Wade Books,
an imprint of Random House Children's Books,
a division of Penguin Random House LLC, New York.

Schwartz & Wade Books and the colophon are trademarks of Penguin Random House LLC.

Visit us on the Web! rhcbooks.com

Educators and librarians, for a variety of teaching tools, visit us at RHTeachersLibrarians.com

Library of Congress Cataloging-in-Publication Data
Names: Zuill, Andrea, author, illustrator.
Title: Sweety / by Andrea Zuill.
Description: First edition. | New York : Schwartz & Wade Books, [2019] |
Summary: Sweety is awkward, even for a naked mole rat, but with encouragement from her Aunt Ruth,
she begins to see that being herself is the best way to find a friend.
Identifiers: LCCN 2018008799 (print) | LCCN 2018015894 (ebook) | ISBN 978-0-525-58002-7 (Ebook)
ISBN 978-0-525-58000-3 (hardcover) | ISBN 978-0-525-58001-0 (library binding)
Subjects: | CYAC: Individuality—Fiction. | Self-confidence—Fiction. | Friendship—Fiction. | Naked mole rat—Fiction. | Rodents—Fiction.
Classification: LCC PZ7.1.Z83 (ebook) | LCC PZ7.1.Z83 Swe 2019 (print) | DDC [E]—dc23

The text of this book is set in P22 Sherwood.
The illustrations were rendered in pen-and-ink, scanned, and colored digitally.
Book design by Rachael Cole

MANUFACTURED IN CHINA
2 4 6 8 10 9 7 5 3 1
First Edition